Leticia pointed up the street and said, "Look at him."

It was Henry Blum. He went to the Falk School, too, but it took him much longer to get home. One of his legs was thin and weak, and it dragged when he walked. He had to use a cane.

"He had polio," Leticia said. "He's a cripple."

Betsy watched as Henry limped slowly up the hill. She had known him all her life, and had never really thought about his leg. It was a part of him, a fact, the way some people had red hair.

That night Betsy couldn't sleep. She kept seeing Henry's hurt face and hearing his bad leg drag on the sidewalk. In her mind, she imagined a scowling little monster with red eyes and fangs who went after children—the polio virus.

Finally she got out of bed and went to the door of her parents' room. She had an important question for them.

She heard her mother say, "We're so close to a vaccine. I just pray it won't be too late. In a way, poor Henry's lucky. He's had polio. He can never get it again. But Betsy and Sam . . ."

Slowly Betsy turned and went back to her room. Her important question had been answered. She'd wanted to ask if she could get polio. Now she knew the answer was yes.

Close to Home

A STORY OF THE POLIO EPIDEMIC

BY LYDIA WEAVER

ILLUSTRATED BY AILEEN ARRINGTON

PUFFIN BOOKS

*I would like to thank the following people for their time and help:
Charles L. Mee, Jr., Fritz Weaver, and Dr. Paul Griner.
Special thanks to Dr. H. Bruce Ostler, who read
this text for background authenticity.*

PUFFIN BOOKS
Published by the Penguin Group
Penguin Books USA Inc., 375 Hudson Street, New York, New York 10014, U.S.A.
Penguin Books Ltd, 27 Wrights Lane, London W8 5TZ, England
Penguin Books Australia Ltd, Ringwood, Victoria, Australia
Penguin Books Canada Ltd, 10 Alcorn Avenue, Toronto, Ontario, Canada M4V 3B2
Penguin Books (N.Z.) Ltd, 182-190 Wairau Road, Auckland 10, New Zealand

Penguin Books Ltd, Registered Offices: Harmondsworth, Middlesex, England

First published in the United States of America by Viking,
a division of Penguin Books USA Inc., 1993
Published in Puffin Books, 1997

1 3 5 7 9 10 8 6 4 2

Text copyright © Lydia Weaver, 1993
Illustrations copyright © Aileen Arrington, 1993
All rights reserved

THE LIBRARY OF CONGRESS HAS CATALOGED THE VIKING EDITION AS FOLLOWS:
Weaver, Lydia.
Close to home: a story of the polio epidemic /
by Lydia Weaver; illustrated by Aileen Arrington.
p. cm.—(Once upon America)
Summary: In the summer of 1952, Betsy sees her vacation fun overshadowed by
the spreading polio epidemic, while her mother and other scientists work
frantically to develop a vaccine for the crippling disease.
ISBN 0-670-84511-6
[1. Poliomyelitis—Fiction.] I. Arrington, Aileen, ill. II. Title. III. Series.
PZ7.W3585C1 1993 [Fic]—dc20 92-25937 CIP AC

Puffin Books ISBN 0-14-036083-2
Printed in the United States of America

ONCE UPON AMERICA® is a registered trademark of Viking Penguin,
a division of Penguin Books USA Inc.

For my goddaughters,
Clara Griner and Marian Gottlieb

Contents

Summer Plans

The classroom window was open. Outside it already felt like summer. Betsy couldn't believe she had to sit at this old desk for another four days. Mrs. Semel had tried to get them to write an essay about what they planned to do during vacation. Most people had written only a few sentences, but Mrs. Semel didn't seem to care very much. Maybe she wished school were over, too.

Betsy looked down at her own paper. *June 19, 1952. I may be called Betsy,* she had written, *but my real name is Elizabeth. Just like the new queen of England. I think the whole point of summer vacation is that you don't have to make any plans!*

Mrs. Semel called on Stuey Hancock. "This summer I will ride my bike," he read out loud. "I will learn to do a wheelie."

Julia Linnell read, "I will help my mother bake a perfect blueberry pie for the Pillsbury Bake-Off."

Then Mrs. Semel called on Leticia Applegate. Even after a whole fifth grade together, the only thing Leticia had ever said to Betsy was, "May I borrow your pencil?" She'd never given it back, either.

Leticia had shiny brown hair that she wore in a neat ponytail. Today it was tied with a silk ribbon that matched her yellow dress. Her dark brown eyes sparkled. All the boys liked Leticia. They pulled her hair and pushed her down in dodgeball. She just stuck out her tongue and laughed. She had a new best girlfriend every week.

"This summer I will take singing lessons. Also ballet," Leticia read. "I will go horseback riding. I will go on a trip. I will stay up till midnight and learn to play bridge. Also to dance the bunny hop."

"My, my," said Mrs. Semel. "You'll be busy."

Then Mrs. Semel pointed to Betsy. After she read her essay, she saw that Leticia was smiling at her. She smiled back. Then they both laughed. For some reason it was very funny that Leticia had a million plans and Betsy had none.

The Falk School was on top of a hill in Pittsburgh, Pennsylvania. When Betsy stood on the playground, she could see all of Pittsburgh in three directions— that is, if there wasn't a cloud of smog from the steel mills. Up here on the hill, Pittsburgh looked like the biggest city in the world. Even bigger than London, where Queen Elizabeth lived.

Leticia stood next to Betsy. She said, "This is such a small town. You and I were meant for more exciting places." She linked her arm through Betsy's. "Want to walk home? Maybe we could be best friends."

Feeling important, Betsy said, "Sure." She and Leticia strolled down the street and started up another small hill. When they got to Bryn Mawr Road, Betsy invited Leticia over for milk and cookies.

"Don't you have Coca-Cola?" Leticia asked.

It turned out that Leticia and her mother lived on Andover Terrace, a block away from Betsy, and lower on the hill. "My father was killed in the Korean War," said Leticia. "He was a brave soldier. He got a hundred medals."

They sat on Betsy's front porch under the awning and sipped their milk. Betsy tried to hold her glass the way Leticia did, with her little finger sticking out. She was glad her younger brother, Sam, was at a friend's house. Sam was seven years old and a pest.

"How come your father's at home and your mother's not?" asked Leticia.

"My father is a reporter for the *Sun-Telegraph*," Betsy answered. "He writes at home. My mother usually works till dinnertime. She's a scientist."

"How strange," Leticia said. Betsy almost felt she should say she was sorry. But for what?

She was relieved when Leticia pointed up the street and said, "Look at *him*."

It was Henry Blum. He went to the Falk School, too, but it took him much longer to get home. One of his legs was thin and weak, and it dragged when he walked. He had to use a cane.

"He had polio," Leticia said. "He's a cripple."

Betsy watched as Henry limped slowly up the hill. She had known him all her life, and had never really thought about his leg. It was a part of him, a fact, the way some people had red hair.

Leticia said, "He got polio because his father is a Communist."

Betsy stared at Henry. A Communist! Communists were bad people who were trying to take over the country. At least she thought so.

Leticia stood up. "Commie!" she called to Henry. "Your daddy's a pinko, so you got polio! Pink-o, po-li-o!"

Henry stopped, surprised. Leticia tugged Betsy's arm. "Pinko, polio," she sang, grinning at Betsy.

Pinko meant "red," and Red was another name for Communist, Besty knew. She had thought the Russians were the Reds. But Henry's father was German. She was confused.

Betsy wanted to please Leticia. "Pinko, polio!" Her voice felt like it was coming from another person. She felt as if she were sitting on the roof of the Methodist church next door, watching herself and Leticia and Henry. Henry's face was turning red.

The front door flew open. Betsy's father stood there. "Girls! Betsy! What do you think you're doing?" He stared at Betsy as if she were a stranger. "Say you're sorry to him! Right now!"

Betsy sputtered out an apology to Henry, who still stood there, mouth open, as if she'd slapped him. She turned to Leticia for support, but Leticia wasn't there. Down the street, Betsy could see the flash of a yellow dress turning into the shortcut to Andover Terrace and disappearing. Only her half-empty milk glass remained.

That night, Betsy's mother didn't get home till Betsy was in bed. She came in and sat down on the edge of the bed, smelling of Chanel No. 5 perfume and some sort of chemical from the lab where she worked.

"No one really knows exactly how you get polio, Betsy," said Mrs. Willmore. "Do you breathe it in? Do you swallow it in food or water? We don't know. That's a problem because people come up with crazy ideas to explain it to themselves. But one thing's for sure. You do not get polio from having a foreign accent or by being different."

"But if Henry's father is a Communist . . . ?"

From the doorway, Betsy's father said, "That's just silly. Mr. Blum is a respected citizen." He sounded angry. "This country's scared of its own shadow," Betsy heard him mutter.

"Anyone can get polio. It's caused by a virus, Betsy," said her mother. "A virus is a tiny little creature that doesn't care who it infects. I'm afraid it seems to pick on children more than anyone else. That's why I go to the lab every day. I'm working with a lot of people who are trying to find a way to stop that virus."

After her parents left her bedroom, Betsy couldn't sleep. She kept seeing Henry's hurt face and hearing his bad leg drag on the sidewalk. In her mind, she imagined a scowling little monster with red eyes and fangs who went after children—the polio virus.

Finally she got out of bed and went to the door of her parents' room. She had an important question for them.

She heard her mother say, "We're so close to a

vaccine. I just pray it won't be too late. In a way, poor Henry's lucky. He's *had* polio. He can never get it again. But Betsy and Sam . . ."

Slowly Betsy turned and went back to her room. Her important question had been answered. She'd wanted to ask if *she* could get polio. Now she knew the answer was yes.

A New Best Friend

Suddenly it seemed the word *polio* was everywhere. Soon there was going to be an election and the country would have a new president. Would it be General Dwight D. Eisenhower or Adlai Stevenson? The Cold War with Russia was going on. And a senator named Joseph McCarthy was finding Communists everywhere.

But polio was what the newspapers reported, or so it seemed to Betsy. Each day they printed how many new cases there were. The summer of 1952 was turning out to be one of the worst polio epidemics ever.

Everywhere you looked, you were reminded. Hanging in the post office, attached to lampposts, in the butcher's window, the grocer's, were the posters. MARCH OF DIMES, they read. SPONSORED BY THE NATIONAL FOUNDATION FOR INFANTILE PARALYSIS. YOUR MONEY CAN HELP HER. And the picture showed a smiling little girl wearing a velvet dress. She was so pretty that you almost didn't notice the steel braces on her legs or the metal crutches she held. Infantile paralysis was the old name for polio, Betsy's mother had explained.

Betsy herself tried hard not to think about it. Maybe if she didn't think about the terrible virus, it would ignore her, too.

One hot day, Leticia appeared at Betsy's house. Betsy was surprised. She thought Leticia had decided not to be her friend. After her father had yelled at them for teasing Henry, she had run away so fast. But Leticia acted as if nothing had happened.

"Like my new sweater?" she asked Betsy, twirling proudly. It was a deep blue-purple and matched Leticia's hair ribbon.

"Aren't you hot?" Betsy asked.

"Well . . . sort of," Leticia admitted. "My mother

makes me wear it. I have to keep warm so I don't get polio."

"You can't get it from being cold!" Betsy remembered what her mother had said about people's crazy ideas.

Leticia shrugged. "Want to come over to my house?" she asked.

Just then, Sam came running into the front yard. He was wearing a Pittsburgh Pirates uniform. He slid in front of them, roaring, "Safe!"

Betsy said, "Sam, get up. That's my little brother," she said to Leticia, rolling her eyes. "He thinks he's Ralph Kiner."

To her surprise, Leticia bent over Sam, who was lying in the dirt. "I can tell you're a *much* better player than Ralph Kiner," she said. "Ralph's a great hitter, but he has no speed."

Sam gazed up at her in wonder.

As they walked down the street toward Andover Terrace Leticia said to Betsy, "Every girl should know a little bit about baseball."

Leticia's house was huge, with white steps leading up to a porch as big as a living room. Betsy said, "Just you and your mother live here?"

"After my father died, my grandfather wanted us near him. He bought us this house. He's rich," Leticia said.

Inside, the furniture was big and dark and gleamingly

polished. A portrait of a handsome soldier who had the same sparkling brown eyes as Leticia hung over the fireplace.

The room reminded Betsy of a museum. Everything was so quiet and untouched. And it was hot. There seemed to be no air in here. "Why don't you open a window or something?" she asked Leticia.

A soft, whispery voice from the doorway answered her. "Oh, no, dear! We must keep out the awful germs!"

Betsy turned. A frail woman in a black dress stood there. Leticia was almost as tall as she was. "Betsy, this is my mother," Leticia said.

"Aren't you the little girl whose father is a reporter?" Leticia's mother asked. Betsy nodded proudly. "And your mother . . . she works, too, doesn't she?"

"She works at the Virus Research Laboratory at the university. They're going to find a way to stop polio."

Mrs. Applegate's big eyes widened. "Oh, don't say that terrible word!" Her hands clasped and unclasped themselves nervously at her waist.

Betsy was flustered. Had she said something wrong?

Mrs. Applegate said, "Your mother must be very brave to work in such a place. I think it's wonderful when women have jobs. Even if they have to leave their children alone all day. Do you ever eat a hot dinner, dear?"

Now Betsy was really confused. Mrs. Applegate seemed to be paying her mother a compliment, only it didn't feel that way. Usually Betsy was proud of her mother's important job. Now she wasn't so sure.

"We're going to play," Leticia said.

"Fine. I'm going to lie down myself, so please do something quiet. Maybe your paint-by-numbers picture of the kittens?"

Upstairs, it was even hotter. In Leticia's pretty pink bedroom, Betsy noticed that her window was also shut tightly. Someone had hammered a nail into the frame so you couldn't open it if you wanted to.

For the next few hours, the girls plunged into a complicated game. Leticia was the leader, giving Betsy directions. At first, Betsy thought Leticia was bossy. Then she began to enjoy herself. Soon she felt as though she were in the middle of the most interesting story she'd ever heard.

The girls pretended they were sisters walking in the woods. Suddenly, the Russians dropped an atom bomb. The girls jumped into a lake, swam to the bottom, and found a passageway to the center of the earth. There they made friends with monsters made of lava. When it was time to go back, they found that everything on earth had been destroyed. Besides them, the only

people alive were James Dean and Marlon Brando. Leticia and Betsy agreed they were the two cutest movie stars.

The girls lay on the floor fanning themselves. Betsy longed for a cold drink, but she didn't want to interrupt the game.

Leticia seemed to think they'd finished, though. She jumped up and pulled a box out of the closet. "Want to see my new shoes?"

She took the lid off the box. Betsy couldn't believe her eyes. The shoes lay on white tissue paper. They were covered with shiny red sequins.

"The ruby slippers!" said Betsy. In *The Wizard of Oz*, Dorothy got the magic shoes when her house fell on the Wicked Witch of the East. The shoes saved her from the Wicked Witch of the West and sent her home at the end.

Here in Leticia's room, the shoes seemed to glow in the afternoon sunlight. Leticia slipped them on. "My mother thinks they're ordinary party shoes. But they're magic, just like the real ruby slippers. Whatever I wish for, I can have."

Betsy almost believed her. It hurt to look at the shoes, they shone so brightly.

"I haven't wished for anything yet," Leticia said, staring down at the shoes. "I'm saving up for a really big wish. I don't know what it is yet. Hey, maybe you can help me decide. You can share it with me. We'll each wish on a shoe."

Betsy was speechless with delight. Leticia held a shoe out to her, and she put it on. "We're the same size!" Betsy said.

"That means we'll be best friends forever," said Leticia.

A Great Idea

The two girls spent most of their time together. Once Betsy asked Leticia about her essay for Mrs. Semel. "What about all those things you were going to do?"

Leticia laughed and said, "Oh, I just made them up so I would sound more interesting than I really am."

Sometimes the girls played at Betsy's house, but it was often too noisy there. Sam and some of his friends had a flying-saucer club. For hours they'd sit on the porch staring up at the sky. Every now and then someone would yell, "I see one!" The whole house would shake as five little boys ran to look.

So the two girls would go to Leticia's, but her house was always so hot that Betsy sometimes got dizzy. And it was too quiet there. Mrs. Applegate was always lying down. They had to be very careful not to bother her. The only reason Betsy liked to go to Leticia's house was to look at the ruby slippers. The girls were still trying to decide about their wishes.

Betsy tried to talk Leticia into playing outside. The hill they lived on was full of underbrush to hide in and trees to climb. But Leticia would look around to see if her mother could hear. She'd say, "My mother doesn't want me to get dirty. You can get polio from mud." Then she'd whisper, "I can't upset her. Since my father died, she's been really nervous."

Betsy asked her mother about polio and mud. "No," said Mrs. Willmore. Then she sighed and said, "At least we don't think so. But you can't stop living your life."

One hot afternoon, Sam and his friends were running around after the neighbor's poodle, Fifi. Sam had heard there was a new dog food you could buy that had chlorophyll in it. He'd saved his money to buy some. Chlorophyll was supposed to have a cool, minty flavor and cure your dog of bad breath. The trouble was, it turned the dog food green and smelled like air freshener. Fifi took one sniff and ran. Sam and his friends pounded after her, laughing and yelling.

Betsy said, "They're driving me crazy. It's so hot! And there's nowhere to go!"

Leticia said, "If we were movie stars, we could sit by my pool and go swimming whenever we wanted. There are no germs in Hollywood."

"As long as there are no little brothers!"

Leticia said, "Oh, I think Sam's cute. He's got a great imagination." Betsy just looked at her.

"Listen, I have an idea," Leticia said. "Let's really go swimming."

Betsy was puzzled. "But we can't. All the swimming pools are closed this summer." That was because of the polio epidemic. Some people thought you got the polio virus from water.

"We'll make our own swimming pool," said Leticia.

"How do we do that? What about your mother?"

"She went shopping with my grandfather. She'll be gone all day. Come on!"

Leticia led Betsy to a large red-brick house a few doors down from hers. She said, "The Jacobsens live here. They're away for the weekend." The girls crept around the house to the backyard. There they saw a large concrete foundation set about six feet into the ground. Building materials, bricks, and sawhorses were scattered around nearby.

"The Jacobsens are building a bomb shelter," Leticia said. "If we filled it up with water, it would make a perfect swimming pool!"

Betsy was shocked. "We'll get in trouble."

"No one will see us. Anyway, we won't fill it *all* the way up. Just enough to cool us off. The Jacobsens will think it rained. No one will ever know."

"Where will we get the water?"

"There's a faucet on the side of the house. We'll carry buckets."

"It will take too long. . . ."

"Are you afraid?" Leticia stared at Betsy.

Betsy was silent. It really was hot. She imagined herself jumping into a cool blue pool of water. How good it would feel.

They found some buckets filled with old chips of paint and bits of wood and plaster, and emptied them.

Soon they were lugging sloshing buckets of water over to the concrete foundation. After they had made about twenty trips, there was only an inch or two of dusty brown water in the bottom.

"We need help," Leticia announced. "I'll get Sam."

"He'll never do it."

"He will if I ask him."

Sure enough, in ten minutes, Leticia was back with Sam and two of his buddies, Tony and Shane. They were excited about the swimming pool. Sam especially seemed eager to show Leticia how big his muscles were.

He staggered back and forth, dragging the full buckets. Leticia, sitting on a sawhorse, said, "Wow, Sam. You are really strong!" Tony and Shane tried harder, too. Betsy just shook her head.

In an hour, there was a foot of brown water in the bottom of the foundation. Dust and paint chips floated on the surface. It certainly didn't look very inviting.

But Leticia said, "Darlings, welcome to my Hollywood mansion!" Then she pulled off the sweater she always wore. Underneath, there was a pretty red halter top that matched her shorts. Gracefully she stepped into the pool. The water came to her knees. Ignoring the paint chips, she sat down, sighing. "Ah. The water's divine. Do join me, Elizabeth."

The water looked like puddles in the gutter after a rainstorm—dirty and oily. But Betsy didn't want to be a spoilsport, so she jumped in, too. The water smelled funny but it was cool, and Betsy had to admit it felt good.

Leticia said to Sam, Tony, and Shane, "You are my three butlers. Please bring us lemonade cocktails immediately."

To Betsy's surprise, the boys played along. They bowed and pretended to bring trays of drinks and food. They said "Yes, ma'am" to Leticia and even called Betsy "Your Majesty" after Leticia told them to.

Finally, Leticia said, "You've been good butlers. You may share my pool."

With whoops of glee, the three boys jumped. They splashed and yelled, and soon there was a water fight going on. Laughing, Betsy and Leticia joined in. In no time, everybody was soaking wet.

Betsy had water in her eyes. She couldn't see, but she noticed that, one by one, the others were falling silent. The water stopped sloshing. She rubbed her eyes and looked.

Mrs. Applegate stood at the edge of the foundation. Her face was very pale. She said in her whispery voice, "Leticia. Oh, my baby. Get out of there. Get out of there now. Now!"

Leticia stood up quickly, dripping. "They made me do it," she said, scrambling out. "I didn't want to. They made me!" Her eyes flashed a message at Betsy. *Forgive me,* they seemed to say, *but I mustn't upset her.*

Betsy and the three boys sat silently in the water. Mrs. Applegate grabbed Leticia by the arm and walked away, her high heels clicking on the cement.

"What Would I Do If . . ."

Every Saturday night, Mr. Willmore brought home a large pizza pie, as a special treat. It cost 75 cents at Luigi's, and it was Betsy and Sam's favorite dinner.

Tonight Betsy could eat only a few bites. She was tired from carrying all those buckets of water through the heat. She was puzzled and angry at what Leticia had done. And she was scared. She kept looking over at Sam. Would he let something slip about their swimming pool?

Part of her wanted to blurt it out to her father and

mother. Even if they were angry, it would be a relief to tell.

But no, she decided. She couldn't tell her parents about the dangerous game they'd been playing. She couldn't bear to see the worry on their faces.

Mrs. Willmore said, "Aren't you hungry, Betsy?"

Maybe Mrs. Applegate herself would come over and tell Betsy's parents. And maybe she'd blame Betsy, even though it had been Leticia's idea!

Betsy stood up. "May I be excused?"

Instantly Mrs. Willmore was on her feet, too. "What's the matter?" She felt Betsy's forehead. "You're very warm," she said, glancing at Mr. Willmore. "It's probably nothing, but I'm going to put you to bed." Betsy could tell she was trying to make her voice light.

As she tucked Betsy in Mrs. Willmore kept asking questions in a casual way—too casual. "Do you have any pains? Does your head hurt? Do you have a sore throat? Is it your stomach?" Betsy wasn't fooled. She saw the fear. She felt it, too. Her stomach did hurt. Her head felt heavy. And her whole body ached.

Light from the hallway spilled onto Betsy's rug. The golden beam looked like the yellow brick road. Betsy's eyes closed. She slept, and dreamed of a line of tiny red-eyed monsters with fangs, dancing toward her down a path of light.

When she woke up, the hallway was dark. She sat up slowly. Her stomach didn't hurt as much, but her shoulders and back were very sore. Her legs throbbed. She thought of Henry Blum.

What would I do if I had a crippled leg? she wondered.

She tried to imagine it. It would take her longer to walk to school. And she'd have to skip gym. No more dodgeball. But maybe she'd get so good at jacks that she could beat anyone, just like Henry Blum.

But how about *two* crippled legs? Betsy pictured the girl in the March of Dimes poster. Did they give you a beautiful dress if you posed for the poster? She'd be famous. Her picture would hang in stores all over the country. If she had to have two crippled legs and metal crutches, maybe it wouldn't be the end of the world.

What if I had to have a wheelchair? Betsy wondered. What would it be like never to walk again?

Well, she thought, if I can't walk, then I'll ride. Her legs would never again get tired from climbing up and down the hills of Pittsburgh. Maybe it wouldn't be so bad.

Then Betsy wondered, What if I couldn't move at all? Her mind stuck at that thought.

She lay back and pretended she couldn't move, to see what it would be like. Her sore muscles began to get worse. Her neck got stiff. She thought she heard a noise in the hallway, but she wouldn't let herself turn her head to look. She wanted to see exactly what it felt like not to be able to move at all.

Betsy thought, Yes, I would still be me. I could still think, and talk, and laugh at jokes. I could still read.

Mrs. Willmore came into the room. She turned on the light beside Betsy's bed. "I thought I heard you calling. Why, sweetheart! Are you crying?"

Betsy looked at her mother. She hadn't realized she was crying, but her cheeks were wet.

Mrs. Willmore laid her hand on Betsy's forehead. "You're much cooler now. I think your fever's gone. How do you feel?"

Betsy sat up slowly. She wiggled her fingers. She curled her toes. Her muscles were still sore, but she could move them. Her stomach had stopped hurting.

Mrs. Willmore was crying, too. "I think you're all right," she said.

Betsy sat on the front porch. Her mother was making her take it easy for a few days, but she felt fine. The wind was from the north, so the smell of smoke from the steel mills wasn't so bad. The sky was bright blue.

Sam came out on the porch carrying his Tom Corbett lunchbox. It was his favorite. It showed handsome Tom Corbett standing in his spaceship. Outside

the spaceship window, you could see rockets firing as the enemy spacemen attacked.

Sam handed it to her. "My Tom Corbett Super-Atomic Gun is inside. You can keep it till you're all better. Hey . . . look who's here."

It was Leticia. She stood on the sidewalk about twenty feet away from the Willmores' house. She called, "Are you better?"

Betsy nodded slowly. She was still mad at Leticia for blaming the swimming pool on her. But maybe Leticia had come to say she was sorry. Maybe they could still be best friends. All at once Betsy decided to forgive her. She said, "Want to come in?"

Leticia didn't move any closer. "I can't. That's what I came over to tell you. I'm not allowed to play with you anymore."

Betsy was angry again. She said, "That swimming pool was *your* idea!"

Leticia said, "It's not that. My mother says your mother brings polio germs home from that place where she works. I might get it from your house."

Betsy said, "But—" Then she was quiet. She couldn't argue with Leticia or her mother. She couldn't argue with any of the other people who thought they knew how you got polio. They would believe what they wanted.

Leticia said, "Well, good-bye." Then she stopped. "See, my mother isn't very strong," she said. "I get into too much trouble. I'm always upsetting her." She shrugged and slowly walked off down the street.

Betsy and Sam watched her disappear down the shortcut to Andover Terrace. Sam said, "I used to like her once, but now I think she's a yo-yo."

But Betsy wasn't mad anymore. Now she just felt sorry for Leticia.

The Magic Shot

The Willmores were in the car, driving to the university. Mrs. Willmore was going to give them a tour of the lab where she worked.

Sam said, "Can we see the monkeys? Can we?"

His parents looked at each other. "Maybe after," said Mrs. Willmore.

After what? Betsy wondered.

Even though it was Saturday, the Virus Research Laboratory was crowded. People bustled up and down the halls carrying test tubes or pushing carts filled with rattly bottles.

At the end of a long hall, Betsy saw a man wearing eyeglasses, talking to a group of people. "That's Dr. Salk," Mrs. Willmore whispered. Betsy knew Dr. Jonas Salk was in charge of the lab. Her mother thought he was very special. "A hero," she had once called him.

Now Mrs. Willmore led them down to the basement. "This is where I work. In those test tubes there's a sort of soup made out of tissue from the human body. We keep those tubes at just the right temperature— not too hot, not too cold—and then we drop in the virus and wait for it to grow."

Betsy backed away a few steps. She was sure that if she looked hard enough, she'd see the little red-eyed, sharp-fanged monster. It would be standing up in the test tube and pointing at her. "I don't like it here," she said.

Her father said, "Don't worry. This is a good place, Betsy."

Mrs. Willmore explained, "When you give someone a vaccination, that means you give them a kind of magic shot. The shot contains a tiny, tiny bit of the virus. The virus in the shot is dead, but when it gets into your bloodstream, your body thinks it's the real thing. So your body quickly gathers all its soldiers and gangs up on the little virus. Then, later, if the real

virus gets in, your body still has those soldiers ready to go. That's called *immunity*."

Betsy saw her mother take two big needles out of a drawer. She poked one into a bottle of clear liquid and drew some of the liquid into it.

"Only a few very lucky people get to try the vaccine right now. Some children at the Watson Home in Sewickley Heights, and at another place called the Polk School. Soon the vaccine will be tested all across the country, and then everybody will be able to have it. But we already know it's safe."

Mrs. Willmore filled the second needle with the clear liquid. Betsy looked at Sam. His eyes were wide. He was watching those needles, too.

Mr. Willmore said, "Your mother has had the shot. Everybody who works here at the lab has, and some of their families."

Betsy's mother said, "If you're a scientist, you some-times want to try things on yourself first. Well, now it's your turn."

Sam said flatly, "I hate shots."

Mr. Willmore said, "I bet Tom Corbett would want you to do it. I bet he'd do it himself."

Sam looked doubtful. Finally he said, "Okay." He stuck out his arm and squeezed his eyes shut.

Betsy was impressed. Her little brother was braver than she was. He let out a small yelp when his mother pricked him with the needle, but he didn't cry.

"Betsy?" her mother said.

After a moment, Betsy drew herself up as tall as she could and held out her arm. She stared at the sharp needle as it came closer and closer.

It stung as it went in. She wouldn't let her breath out as long as that needle was in there.

Finally it was over. She felt a little shaky, but she didn't cry, either. Mr. Willmore said, "You had such a funny look on your face. What were you thinking?"

"I was pretending I was Queen Elizabeth," Betsy said.

Sam said again, "I want to see the monkeys!"

Mrs. Willmore sighed. "This is not a zoo, Sam."

"What monkeys?" Betsy wanted to know.

"They come from India. They live here," Sam explained. "Mom, I think we should bring one home. He could sleep in my room. I'd name him Tom."

Mrs. Willmore looked away. "They are not pets. We don't call them *he* or *she*. A monkey is an *it*. I don't think we can visit them today. Listen, I'll meet you out front." She hurried down the hall.

Mr. Willmore turned to the children. "The scientists who work here try not to get too fond of the monkeys. But it's hard because they're so cute. That's why your mother snapped at you."

Betsy said, "Wait a minute. They're giving the monkeys polio, aren't they? They're using them for *tests*."

"That's right, Betsy. The monkeys have helped the scientists make the vaccine safe."

Betsy was quiet on the way home. They bought ice cream cones and ate them in the car, but hers didn't have much taste. Polio. All she could think about was polio. How could there be such an awful disease? It hurt people. It hurt animals. It was horrible and unfair.

She stared out the window, rubbing the sore spot on her arm where the needle had gone in. She wished she lived somewhere far away where they'd never heard of polio. But she knew no such place existed.

The car sat at a red light. Sam said, "There's that cuckoo Leticia."

She was skipping rope by herself on the sidewalk in front of her house. When she saw their car, she backed up a bit, as if the car itself could give her germs.

Sam leaned out the window and yelled, "We've been vac-ci-nated!" He could barely pronounce the word, but he said it proudly. "Now we can't get polio! *Nyah-nyah!*"

"Sam!" Mrs. Willmore said. "We're not supposed to tell people yet. Not until everyone can have the vaccine."

"Especially not in such a nasty way!" As Mr. Willmore drove on down the street, shaking his head, Betsy looked out the back window.

Leticia was staring after their car. She looked lonely and a bit scared.

Close to Home

A loud wailing sound woke Betsy out of a deep sleep. For a minute, she thought it was an air raid. She jumped out of bed, putting her arms over her head the way she'd been taught to do in school in case of a bomb. As she sat on the floor, heart pounding, she slowly realized it wasn't an air raid, after all. It was just a regular siren.

Where was it coming from? She ran to the window. Through the trees covering the hillside, she could see a flashing red light on the road below hers, Andover

Terrace. From her bedroom window, she saw her father step out into the street. Betsy grabbed her bathrobe. If her father could go look, so could she.

She slipped out of the house into the cool darkness. The sound of the siren filled the night. She could see lights going on in houses up and down the block. People in bathrobes appeared at front doors.

"Betsy!" her mother called from her bedroom window above. "Betsy, come back inside!"

But Betsy was drawn toward the wailing siren and the flashing red light. She knew where the shortcut to Andover Terrace was so well that she could have found it blindfolded. It was strange to be running down the stone stairs in the middle of the night, though.

When she stepped onto Andover Terrace, she saw her father. She ran over to him. He said, "Oh, Betsy, Betsy. This one hits close to home."

The ambulance sat in the road, siren howling. Betsy's heart started to pound again. The ambulance was parked in front of Leticia's house.

The front door opened. Several men dressed in white came out, carrying a stretcher. On the stretcher lay a still form. It was Leticia.

Mrs. Applegate hurried after the stretcher. Even though it was a hot summer night, she wore a heavy wool coat. Her face looked as white as marble in the darkness.

They put Leticia in the ambulance. Mrs. Applegate

climbed in after her, and the doors were shut. The ambulance made a U-turn on the street and drove off very fast down the hill.

Even when the siren faded, Betsy imagined she could still hear it. Her ears ached with the noise, though there was only the sound of crickets around them. "Dad, what was wrong with her?"

"I'm not sure. She was very sick. Maybe . . ."

He didn't have to say it. Betsy knew. What else could it be?

Polio.

Yes, it was polio. The whole neighborhood was talking about it. And Leticia wasn't the only one. Three blocks away, another little boy had gotten it, and had been rushed to the hospital, too.

Betsy sat on the front porch. She didn't feel like playing. She kept looking at her arm where she'd gotten the vaccination. For a few days afterward the spot had been sore and red, but that had gone away. Now, a week later, all you could see was a tiny red dot. She put her finger over the dot and held it there. She felt as if a fairy godmother had touched her with a wand.

Just then, a taxi pulled up in front of the Willmores' house. A tiny woman wearing a heavy coat got out. It was Mrs. Applegate.

Betsy stood up. Mrs. Applegate had come to blame her for giving Leticia polio.

But Mrs. Applegate hurried up the walk and climbed the front steps without even looking at Betsy. She knocked on the door with a flurry of anxious taps. Betsy sat on the steps, trying to look as small as possible. She wanted to find out how Leticia was, but she was afraid to ask.

Mrs. Willmore answered the door. It was Sunday, her day off. She started to say a surprised hello, but Mrs. Applegate interrupted her. "Please . . . I must speak with you."

When the front door closed behind them, Betsy crept around through the bushes to the side of the house. She crouched under the living room window, which was wide open to let in a breeze. It was wrong to listen to a private talk, but she had to hear what Mrs. Applegate was going to say. She was afraid Mrs. Applegate would tell her mother about the swimming pool.

Instead she heard Mrs. Applegate say, "Please . . . please help me."

"Of course," said Mrs. Willmore. "Would you like me to run an errand while you're at the hospital? We are all so sorry—"

"I need the medicine!" Mrs. Applegate said in a desperate whisper.

After a silence, Betsy's mother said, "I don't understand."

"I have plenty of money. I'm willing to pay whatever you ask."

"Mrs. Applegate, I don't know what you're talking about."

"The polio medicine! You work at that lab. I've heard things . . . I know you have it. My poor baby is so sick. I can't lose her, too. I'll be all alone. I know you have the cure!"

Once again there was a silence. Betsy raised her head as far as she dared and saw Mrs. Applegate leaning forward, staring at her mother, nervously clasping and unclasping her hands.

Mrs. Willmore looked very upset. She said slowly, "I know how you feel. I would do anything to save my children, too, but—"

"Then you'll help me?"

"I'm afraid you've misunderstood. There is no polio medicine. There is no cure."

"But I was told—"

"There will soon be a vaccine. It will help *prevent* polio."

Mrs. Applegate rose. "Then give me the vaccine!"

"It won't work for Leticia. Once you have the disease, it's too late. I'm sorry."

"What am I going to do?" Mrs. Applegate whispered. She began to cry. "I tried my best to protect her."

Betsy's mother came forward and put her arms around Mrs. Applegate. Betsy sank back down on her knees in the cool dirt.

After a minute, she heard Mrs. Applegate say, "This is like a bad dream. I will pray with all my heart that your little boy and girl stay healthy."

"Thank you," said Mrs. Willmore. To Betsy, her mother's voice sounded shaky.

Soon, Betsy heard the front door slam. She heard the *click-click* of Mrs. Applegate's high heels on the sidewalk. She heard the car door close. Through the bushes, she saw the taxi pull away from the curb and disappear.

A Visit and a Wish

Stuey Hancock read his essay out loud. "During my summer vacation, I learned to do a wheelie on my bike. I also got seven stitches in my leg."

Julia Linnell read what she had written. "Even though I didn't win the Pillsbury Bake-Off for blueberry pie, I learned how to make a Lady Baltimore cake. Also how to change my baby brother's diaper."

Betsy's piece of paper was blank. She didn't know what to write. "I didn't get polio," was all she could think of. Luckily the new teacher, Mr. Frank, didn't call on her.

After school, she went and stood on the playground and looked out over the city. It seemed like a hundred years ago that she and Leticia had stood here together and started to be friends.

Betsy thought about Leticia a lot. She was bossy. She could be mean. Sometimes she lied. But there had been a sparkle in her eyes. It was exciting to be around her. She was fun. Betsy missed her.

Leticia had been in the hospital for two months. Betsy often wondered what that must be like. She knew a hospital could be a scary place. She decided to ask her parents if she could visit Leticia.

On the way home, Betsy caught up with Henry Blum. "Hi," she said.

He looked at her shyly. Maybe he thought she was going to tease him again.

"What's it like?" she asked him. "Having polio?"

He saw she wasn't being mean. He thought for a minute. "People think that if you can't move your leg, you can't feel pain in it. But you can. It hurts a lot."

"Henry, what do you think will happen to Leticia?"

"She might be just the way she was before. Maybe you won't be able to tell she ever had it."

"Really?"

"Maybe. But maybe not. Maybe she'll end up like me."

Betsy said, "You mean she'll play a great game of jacks?"

Henry was surprised. Then he laughed. So did Betsy. Slowly they walked on down the hill.

Betsy and her father went to the hospital together. Even though Betsy's parents had told her what to expect, Betsy couldn't help being nervous. Everywhere she looked, white-coated doctors and nurses seemed to be washing their hands.

They were going to the floor where the people who were recovering from polio were. There was no fear that Betsy and her father would be exposed to the disease. Even so, Betsy kept reminding herself that she'd had the vaccine.

Betsy couldn't help peeking into rooms as they walked down the hall. Once she saw a boy trying to walk on crutches. A nurse walked with him, holding his arm. In the corner a little girl was wrapping wet washcloths around a doll and telling it, "This will make you well."

Betsy heard a strange sound. It was a kind of *whoosh*. She knew she'd been hearing it since she got off the elevator, but it grew louder and louder as they walked down the hall. Finally they passed the room where the sound was coming from.

Betsy looked in. There was a steel tube about six feet long where the bed should have been. There were windows in the tube, and you could see a boy was lying inside it. His head stuck out one end and rested on a pillow.

"That's called an iron lung, Betsy," her father whispered. "The muscles in that little boy's chest are paralyzed, so his lungs can't move. Using air pressure, the machine breathes for him."

Betsy stared. There was a mirror over the little boy's head. She glanced at it and realized that he was looking back at her, watching the world go by in his mirror. Timidly she smiled. He smiled back as the machine hissed and sighed.

At the very end of the hall there was a large, sunny room. When they entered, Betsy saw Leticia sitting and looking out the window.

"Leticia," she said. Her voice came out a scared squawk.

But Leticia didn't notice the squawk. She turned and grinned. "Well, if it isn't Queen Elizabeth!" she cried. Only then did Betsy see that she was sitting in a wheelchair.

Mr. Willmore said, "I'm going to go find a cup of coffee. You girls have a chat."

After he left, Betsy felt shy. What should she say? She kept looking at the metal wheelchair. Leticia's legs were covered with a pretty plaid blanket. Sure enough, her hair ribbon matched it.

She was thinner than Betsy remembered, and very

pale. There were dark circles under her eyes. Betsy asked, "Does it hurt?"

"Yes," Leticia said flatly. "Especially when they wrap you in steaming-hot towels. That's so your muscles won't get stiff."

That's what that little girl had been doing to her doll, Betsy realized. "My mother said you were getting well."

"I am getting well. I just can't walk yet."

"Oh," Betsy whispered.

"I have a physical therapist. That's a person who makes you do horrible exercises. I call him Teddy the Torturer. He moves my legs around and taps a spot and says, 'Think here.' And I have to shut my eyes and think hard about my toes, to try to move them. So far I can't," she finished matter-of-factly.

"Teddy the Torturer?"

"Oh, he's not really. In fact, he's cute as anything! He likes me. This is where my knowledge of baseball comes in handy."

"I brought you a Nancy Drew book." Betsy held out a wrapped package.

"Oh, good. I do a lot of reading here."

"When are you getting out?"

"Soon. Only I'm not going home. I'm going to a place called Warm Springs. It's in Georgia. President Franklin D. Roosevelt started it. It's only for people who had polio. *He* had polio, you know."

50

"What will you do there?"

"Oh, more horrible exercises." She sounded so carefree. Betsy didn't know whether to believe her or not.

Leticia said, "I *am* going to walk again. Want to know how I know?" Grinning, she lifted up a corner of the plaid blanket. She was wearing the ruby slippers!

"I just look at these and make a wish. A hundred wishes, but they're all the same wish. I hope you don't mind that I used yours up."

"I would have wished for the same thing," Betsy said.

Betsy asked Leticia if they could write letters to each other. Leticia said sure, but Betsy wondered if they really would.

Finally Mr. Willmore stuck his head in the door and said it was time to go. They said good-bye, and Betsy and her father turned to leave. At the door, Betsy looked back.

Leticia was sitting in the sun, looking out the window. A corner of the plaid blanket had fallen away and one of the ruby slippers peeked out. Red sparks glinted on the walls and the metal rims of the wheelchair.

Betsy suddenly knew Leticia was going to be fine. Even if she had a limp, like Henry, she'd find a way to make the best of it. If she had to have crutches, she'd wear a velvet dress and pose for a poster. If she

had to stay in the wheelchair, she'd roll faster than anyone could run.

She would still be herself. It would always be fun to be around her. Betsy would miss her.

All the way down the hall, Betsy kept touching her upper arm where she'd gotten the shot, the magic vaccine.

ABOUT THIS BOOK

By 1962, Dr. Salk's vaccine had been replaced by one developed by Dr. Albert Sabin. You swallow your vaccine now, instead of getting a shot. It can be stored for longer periods of time and produced less expensively.

Since the Sabin vaccine uses a live virus, the immunity it provides spreads from person to person, and lasts much longer. The immunity provided by the Salk vaccine only lasts about a year. After that you need another shot. Though Dr. Salk's vaccine came first, both men are considered heroes for their contributions.

Thanks to these scientists, we have almost completely gotten rid of polio in the United States. In certain developing countries, however, polio is still a problem. Under some conditions (because of hot climates with poor refrigeration facilities, for instance), the vaccine doesn't work as well. Doctors and scientists are hard at work on solutions. Someday they hope polio will be completely gone from the world.

While I was writing this book, I spoke to several people who had had polio as children. The struggle with the disease changed them and shaped their lives.

One person told me how terribly angry he'd felt at finding himself suddenly paralyzed. The week before, he'd been a football hero at school. His anger made him determined to fight. Today he walks—with crutches, but he walks.

I also spoke to one woman who, as a little girl, had been a Polio Pioneer. That meant she was one of the first to be given the new vaccine. She told me how special she had felt, how proud she had been to be helping other children.

Today we are facing another disease with no cure: AIDS. It, too, is caused by a virus. Viruses are very democratic—that means they will pick on *anybody*.

In the book, Leticia mistakenly thinks that Henry got polio because his father is a foreigner and different from her. But someone who is sick with a disease caused by a virus is just like us—only not so lucky.

The story of polio has a happy ending. Because of the vaccine, the disease is now mostly preventable. Someday scientists will develop a vaccine for AIDS, the way they did for polio. That will be a happy ending, too.

L. W.